BONICI

Library of Congress Cataloging-in-Publication Data:
Oram, Hiawyn.
The Second Princess / by Hiawyn Oram : illustrated by Tony Ross.
p.   cm.
Summary: The Second Princess tries to get rid of her sister, the
First Princess, until she learns that her parents love them both equally.
$13.95
[1. Sibling rivalry—Fiction.   2. Sister—Fiction.
3. Princesses—Fiction.]   I. Ross, Tony, ill. II. Title.
PZ7.0624Se 1994   [E]—dc20 94-1658   CIP   AC

THE SECOND PRINCESS

HIAWYN ORAM + TONY ROSS

ARTISTS & WRITERS GUILD BOOKS
Golden Books
Western Publishing Company, Inc.

Once there were two princesses, the First Princess and the Second Princess.
The First Princess liked being first, but the Second Princess did not like being second.

So the Second Princess ran into the woods to find the Gray Wolf.

"Gray Wolf, Gray Wolf," she said, "you must come to the palace in the dead of night and gobble up my sister so that I can be first."

"Goodness gracious," said the Gray Wolf, "what a wicked thought. I would never do a thing like that. Never."

So the Second Princess went to find the Brown Bear.

"Brown Bear, Brown Bear," she said, "you must come to the palace and marry my sister so she'll have to move away from home and I can be first."

"Oh, must I, indeed?" said the Brown Bear. "Well, let me tell you, I wouldn't marry your sister if she were the last person on earth. Besides, as you can see, I'm already happily married."

So the Second Princess stomped into the palace kitchen.

"Cook, Cook," she said, "bake her in a pie or flip her like a pancake, I don't care.
I want my sister out of the way so I can be first—and that's an order."

"Very well," said the Cook, "but I shall want something in return."

"Like what?" said the Second Princess.

"Jewels," she said with a greedy grin. "I want your mother's jewels. All of them. Jewels, jewels, and more jewels!"

"I'll try," said the Second Princess.

So the Second Princess crept into her mother's bedroom and took what she could
... cramming and stuffing and pocketing glittering gorgeous things ...

lockets, tiaras and watches, necklaces, chokers and chains, bracelets, brooches and earrings, hatpins, buckles and rings ... and though her heart was beating like a loud clock and her knees were trembling like jelly, she grew so busy with all her mother's jewels ...

she did not notice the Maid come in to make the bed, the Queen come in to find the Maid,

two Ladies-in-Waiting come in to find the Queen, two Guards come in to find the Ladies-in-Waiting,

the Lord High Chamberlain come in to find the Guards, and the King come in to find the Lord High Chamberlain.

In fact, only when the Maid sobbed, the Queen gasped, the Ladies-in-Waiting fainted, the Guards shouted, "Who goes there?" and the King marched her off to the Throne Room did the Second Princess realize she was caught — red-handed.

"Well," said the King, wondering why his daughter had been in the Queen's bedroom. "I am waiting, I am waiting, I am waiting."

But, of course, the one thing in the world the Second Princess could NEVER do was TELL what she had been doing with the Queen's jewels.

All she could do was hang her head and try not to imagine what would happen to her if anyone ever found out.

At last the Queen swept in with an idea.

"If you cannot tell us what you were doing with the jewels," she said, "then we shall have to guess. Was it to polish them?"

The Second Princess shook her head.

"Was it to play Kings and Queens with your sister?" said the King.
The Second Princess shook her head.
"Did you want to give the jewels to someone," asked the Queen, "in return for something you wanted ... very, very much?"

Then and only then did the Second Princess put her hands over her eyes so she could only half be seen and whisper so softly through her fingers that the King and Queen had to come very close to hear.

"Yes …" came the soft whisper. "To … be … first."

And to her great surprise the sky did not fall in and the world did not come to an end. Instead the Queen sighed gratefully and the King said, "Thank goodness we know. Now run along and help Mother put away her tiaras ...

"and from now on you will be first on Mondays, Wednesdays, and Fridays," which she was,

"and the First Princess will be first on Tuesdays, Thursdays, and Saturdays,"
which she was,

"and on Sundays we'll all be first," said the King. And they were.

And though the First Princess took a while getting used to not being first all of the time, and the Second Princess took a while getting used to being first some of the time, and Sundays were always a tug-of-war, they all lived happily ever after,

except for the greedy Cook, who stormed off in a huff because all she wanted was jewels, jewels, and more jewels, and because she never knew which day of the week it was, anyway.